The subject matter and vocabulary have been selected with expert assistance, and the brief and simple text is printed in large, clear type.

Children's questions are anticipated and facts presented in a logical sequence. Where possible, the books show what happened in the past and what is relevant today.

Special artwork has been commissioned to set a standard rarely seen in books for this reading age and at this price.

Full-colour illustrations are on all 48 pages to give maximum impact and provide the extra enrichment that is the aim of all Ladybird Leaders.

INDEX

For teachers' use, a map and geographical index is given at the back of the book.

A Ladybird Leader

baby
animals

written and illustrated by John Leigh-Pemberton

Ladybird Books Loughborough

Helpless babies

Some baby animals, such as mice, are born without hair.

Field mouse

Their eyes are closed.
They open after fourteen days.

Other baby animals, like cats and dogs, are born with hair.

Their eyes are closed for nine days.

Babies like these are helpless at first.

Helpless baby animals are usually born
in a nest or a den or a burrow.

There they are kept hidden.

Their mothers look after them.

Even large animals, like this bear,
have cubs which are helpless at first.

When born they are very small.

They stay in the den for a few months.

The young of hunting animals

All animals which hunt other animals
have babies which are helpless.

This serval
is an African cat.

She is carrying
one of her kittens.

Litters

This polecat has four or five young.
They are called a litter.

Size of litters

Different sorts of animals
have different sized litters.

Bears have small families.
Animals such as hamsters sometimes
have large ones.

Babies that are not helpless

Animals which have hooves,
and eat grass, do not make nests.
Young deer, cattle and antelopes
are born among grass and bushes
or in the open.

For a few days this new-born gazelle
will be kept hidden.

European bison
with calf

The young of cattle
are born with their eyes open.

They are born covered with fur.

In a few minutes they can stand.

Running

Animals with hooves
run to escape from enemies.
The young must be able to run too.
This baby gnu runs with its mother.

The herd

Antelopes, horses, and cattle
live in groups.

These are called herds.

A baby must be able
to keep up with the herd.

Zebra and foal

Hiding

Roe deer
and fawns

Mother deer hide their young
in thick grass or bracken.

Most kinds of baby deer
have spotted fur.

This makes them hard to see.

Climbing

Chamois
(*Sham-wa*)

Mountain animals, such as chamois,
must be able to climb
soon after they are born.
They must follow their mother
so that she can feed them.

Brush-tailed possum

The smallest babies

When some animals are born
they are very small indeed.

The possum is one of these.

The mother possum is as large
as a cat.

 But this is the size
of a new-born possum.

The pouch

The mother kangaroo, like the possum, has a flap of skin on her stomach.
This flap makes a pouch.

The young stay in the pouch
until they have grown quite big.

Where animals with pouches live

Many kinds of animals with pouches live in Australia and South America.

Pouched mouse

There is even this 'pouched' mouse in Australia.

Large families

Some pouched animals
have many babies.

Australian native cats often have
more than twenty at a time.

No more than eight grow up.

Small families

The Australian koala has a pouch.
It has one very small baby at a time.

The baby spends six months
in its mother's pouch.
Then it rides on her back.

Where are young animals born?

Baby animals are born
in different sorts of places.

Some animals, such as rabbits,
make a tunnel in the ground.

It is called a burrow.

Burrows

Badger's burrows are called sets.

The nest inside the set
is lined with grass and bracken.

Badger cubs are born blind
and with silvery fur.

Nests

A dormouse

Like birds, some animals make nests.
This one makes a special breeding nest.
It is made of grass, moss
and honeysuckle bark.

The squirrel's drey

A squirrel makes a nest of sticks
and moss.
It looks like a large bird's nest.
It is called a drey.

Nests that are borrowed

A pine marten

Old nests of birds are used
by some animals.
Some martens use them.
Other martens make nests among rocks

Dens

Like this skunk, other animals have dens.
A den is a hiding place for the young.
It may be in a cave
or under the roots of a tree.

Rabbits

Baby rabbits are born in a burrow.
They are blind and helpless
and without fur.
They can run after two weeks.

Hares

Baby hares are called leverets.
They are born in a grassy hollow.
This is called a form.
Their eyes are open.
They have thin fur and can run
as soon as they are born.

Animals born in the snow

Polar bear cubs are born in a den
dug in the snow.

At birth, the cubs are the size of rats.

Animals born in the water

Baby whales and dolphins
are born under water.

As soon as they are born
the mother pushes them to the top.

There, like all whales, they can breathe.

Pilot whale
and calf

Feeding

All the animals in this book
feed their young with milk.
Animals which do this are mammals.

Birds, reptiles and fish
do not feed their young on milk.

How baby animals feed

Young animals suck the milk
from their mother's teats.

Animals which have large litters
have many teats.

Animals with small families
have only two teats.

A pig can feed
twelve piglets at once.

Rich milk

Seals give very thick, oily milk
to their young.
This gives the pups
a layer of fat, called blubber.

Weaning

Some baby animals feed on milk
until they are more than a year old.
Others change to solid food
after a few weeks.
This change of food is called weaning.

Foals are weaned after five months.

Protection

Nearly all mother animals
protect their young.

Sometimes both parents
will defend them bravely.

Rhinos have one calf at a time.
The mother will get between
her calf and any danger.
She will even fight a tiger
which tries to take her calf.

Cleaning baby animals

Mother animals lick their babies
to clean them.
Many animals have rough tongues
to do this.

Lioness and cub

Soon, the young
learn to clean themselves.

Shelter

Young animals must be kept warm and dry.

The musk ox shelters its new-born calf under its long fur.

Fathers

Sometimes, only the mother
brings up her young.
Sometimes the father helps.
He brings food to the mother and young.

Foxes

Marmosets
are small monkeys.
They live in South America.
The mother feeds the babies.
The father carries them about
and washes them.

Knowing how and learning how

Baby animals can do some things
without being shown.
Knowing how to do things
without being shown
is called instinct.

Young otters must learn to swim.
They suck milk by instinct.

A baby animal knows it must follow
its mother.

It knows by instinct.

It knows animals of its own kind
when it sees them, when it smells them
and when it hears them.

A reindeer calf follows its mother.

Eating by instinct

Some animals live together in herds.
These animals do most things by instinc
They do not have to learn to hunt.
They eat leaves or grass.

A buffalo calf follows the herd.

Learning

Animals which hunt
have to teach their young to hunt.

Even when they are playing,
young animals are learning to hunt.

A stoat family goes hunting.

Wolves sometimes live in groups.

They teach their cubs to hunt.

The cubs learn to track
and kill their prey.

Wolves are very intelligent animals.

Groups of wolves have rules.

The cubs must keep to these rules.

They learn to be part of a group.

Talking

Animals do not 'talk' with words.

An animal's smell, sounds
and movements have meanings
for another animal.

Young animals must learn
what all these mean.

A sheep calls
to its lamb.